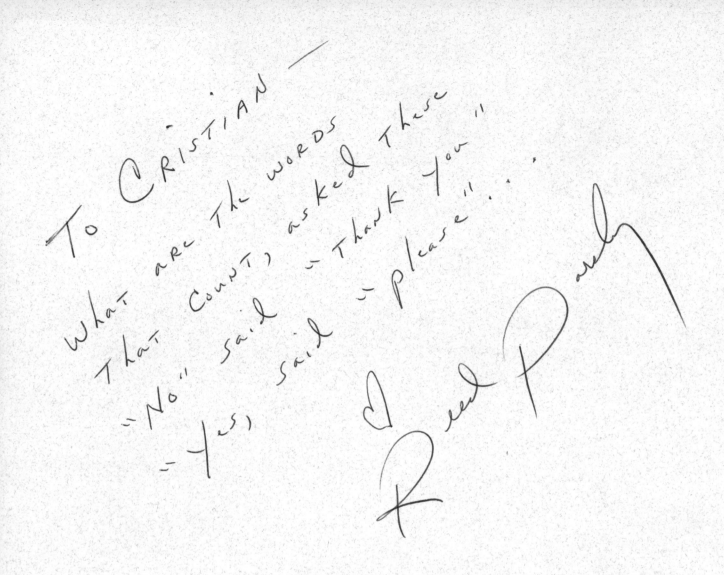

To CRISTIAN —

What are the words
that count? asked these
"No" said "Thank You"
"Yes" said "please"...

Read, Darling

R

Sugar Ships

by Reed Parsley & illustrations by Sparky Fox

GREEN TIGER PRESS
Published by Simon & Schuster
New York London Toronto Sydney Tokyo Singapore

GREEN TIGER PRESS
Simon & Schuster Building, Rockefeller Center, 1230 Avenue of the Americas,
New York, New York 10020.
Text copyright © 1990 by Reed Parsley.
Illustrations copyright © 1990 by Sparky Fox
All rights reserved including the right of reproduction in whole or in part in any form.
GREEN TIGER PRESS is an imprint of Simon & Schuster.
Designed by Judythe Sieck
Manufactured in the United States of America.

10 9 8 7 6 5 4 3 2

Library of Congress Cataloging-in-Publication Data
Parsley, Reed. Sugar ships / by Reed Parsley : illustrated by Sparky Fox.   p.   cm.
Summary: The sugar ships sail the seas on chocolate chips,
leaving only memories in Candy Bay.
[1. Boats and boating—Fiction.   2. Stories in rhyme.]   I. Fox, Sparky, ill.   II. Title.
[PZ8.3.P2588Su   1991]   [E]—dc20   91-16984

ISBN 0-671-74956-0

SUGAR SHIPS

Where are all the sugar ships
That sail the seas on chocolate chips

They take their sweets
And drift downstream

Towards hidden harbors
They drift on dreams

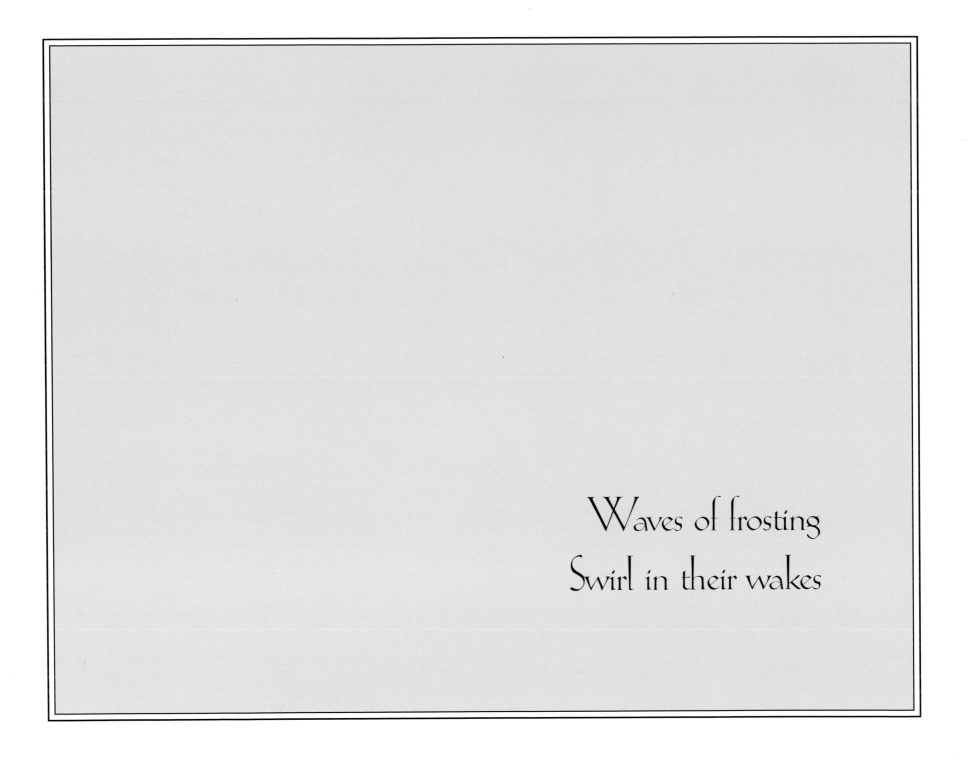

Waves of frosting
Swirl in their wakes

When they pass a tall lighthouse

Made from short cakes

Sugar ships, sugar ships
Around the next bend

What do you look for
The search for an end

See the sugar Clippership

That clips the level rye

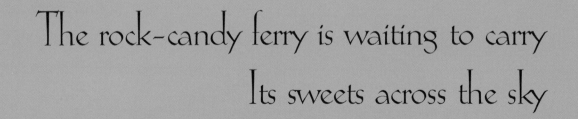

The rock-candy ferry is waiting to carry

Its sweets across the sky

Sugar ships of yellow
Ships of blue and green

Secret sugar ships of white

Sail away unseen

Into inkspilled night they sail

Dark licorice stains

Cleaned up at first light

By light sugar rains

Hear the ships sing out
Hear their bells clang

As they sail past the
Cliffs of Lemon Meringue

All the world's sugar ships
On the edge of ocean's dime

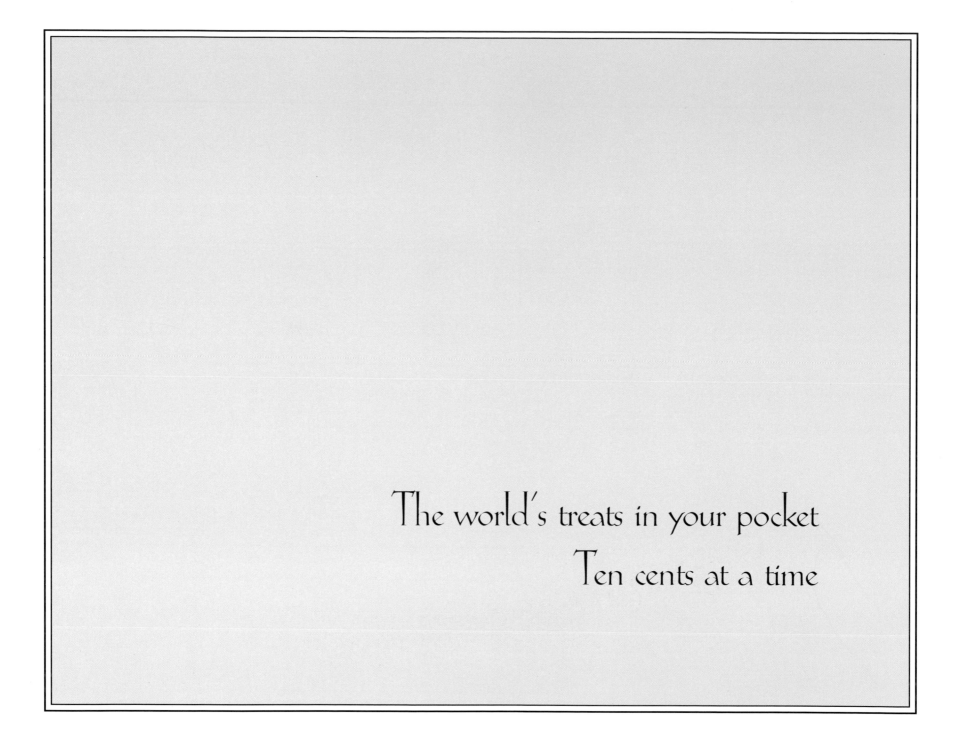

The world's treats in your pocket

Ten cents at a time

Where are all the sugar ships
That sail the seas on chocolate chips

Ahead they spot their final port of call

Sail silently under the Gumball Waterfall

Now all the sugar ships must leave
Growing smaller as they sail away

Leaving but a memory
In forgotten Candy Bay